Peter White lives on the scenic Bay of Plenty coast of New Zealand. He is an acclaimed sports journalist, and travel and magazine writer, with a double degree in English and History and a diploma in journalism. Peter fell in love with England, its history, sport and music, during four life-changing years in the 1980s and 1990s. Hearing Sam Fender for the first time sparked a renewed belief in music's inherent ability to change lives and inspired a creative surge of writing. This is Peter's first published book.

To my dad Maurice, who is a daily inspiration to me and all my family, and my wonderful sister Chris. Thank you for everything.

A special shout out to Dan Sheridan, for encouraging me to keep going with this project. A top journalist and a top bloke.

Peter White

SEVENTEEN GOING UNDER

Short Stories by Peter White

AUSTIN MACAULEY PUBLISHERS™

LONDON • CAMBRIDGE • NEW YORK • SHARJAH

Copyright © Peter White 2024

The right of Peter White to be identified as author of this work has been asserted by the author in accordance with sections 77 and 78 of the Copyright, Designs and Patents Act 1988.

All rights reserved. No part of this publication may be reproduced, stored in a retrieval system, or transmitted in any form or by any means, electronic, mechanical, photocopying, recording, or otherwise, without the prior permission of the publishers.

Any person who commits any unauthorised act in relation to this publication may be liable to criminal prosecution and civil claims for damages.

This is a work of fiction. Names, characters, businesses, places, events, locales, and incidents are either the products of the author's imagination or used in a fictitious manner. Any resemblance to actual persons, living or dead, or actual events is purely coincidental.

A CIP catalogue record for this title is available from the British Library.

ISBN 9781398480568 (Paperback)
ISBN 9781398482418 (Hardback)
ISBN 9781398490147 (ePub e-book)

www.austinmacauley.com

First Published 2024
Austin Macauley Publishers Ltd®
1 Canada Square
Canary Wharf
London
E14 5AA

Sam Fender, please never change. We love you just the way you are. It may not be possible yet for you to know how many lives you have changed for the good, or what a catalyst you have been to rejuvenate the tired old music industry.

Not silly love songs, nor trite rhyming lyrics that make no sense, but songs from inside your core that face up to darker issues most artists prefer to ignore. And great melodies and a voice that transcends the ages.

I was lucky to know what The Jam and The Clash meant to me when I was young and vulnerable. Your songs and impact are just as important today and may end up surpassing them. Paul Weller would be the first to agree.

I was fortunate to see you and your excellent band play in Melbourne in November 2022. It was the best live music experience I have had. Your songs touched everyone there on a far deeper level than just being good tunes to dance to. It was a spiritual encounter. It was special.

This book is for all of us who made it through the night.

Table of Content

Leave Fast	**11**
Seventeen Going Under	**21**
Paradigms	**30**
Spit of You	**43**
Will We Talk	**51**
Mantra	**63**
The Dying Light	**69**
Angel in Lothian	**78**

Leave Fast

Roaring along the Beehive Road. It's a rite of passage for many young guys with their first car that makes a lot of noise and can really shift. The problem is the road can be dangerous for inexperienced drivers, particularly in the wet, with tight corners catching out many over the years. There have been far too many fatalities and serious injuries but every Friday and Saturday night, you can't miss the unmistakable sound of souped-up cars flying around the bends on their own private racetrack.

Beehive Road is not its proper legal name but everyone knows it as that. Hartley Lane, or the B1325, is its official moniker. It runs behind the Beehive, an old-fashioned 18-century pub that is known for great Sunday roasts. The Beehive was Andrew, Rusty, Joey and Smithy's favourite haunt since they were old enough to drink legally at 18. They all grew up together, played football and cricket in the same teams and celebrated their 21st birthdays with one massive party. Joey's dad used to call them The Four Amigos after the American band from the 1960s he liked. The name stuck.

Their good mate Nicholas Meloni supplied the drinks for the 21st party at discount rates. He was an eccentric character who ran an off-license and had been serving the boys since they were 16. Originally from Italy, he was a massive AC Milan fan. His little shop was full of scarves, team jerseys and photos of players.

Nicholas always gave the boys a warm welcome.

'Here they are, The Four Amigos, Whitley Bay's own boy band,' was his usual taunt. They loved to banter with him about football and when he was finally going to change his allegiance to Newcastle. There was no budging him.

'No bloody way, boys. AC Milan is in my heart. You will never convert me,' he always said, laughing.

And then the laughter stopped. The next time Andrew, Rusty and Joey saw their Italian friend was at Smithy's funeral. He was killed two weeks after the memorable 21st party when he missed a corner on the Beehive Road and crashed into a tree. Rusty was meant to go with him but had decided to stay at the Beehive for an extra pint.

Smithy's death ripped the heart out of the group, their families and community. The boys had been inseparable since they were 10. Their parents treated all the boys like their own. It was going to take some time to get over this.

The police report stated the main cause of the accident was excessive speed on the greasy surface after heavy rain showers. Smithy only had one pint, as he was not feeling very well. Who knows whether his headache had anything to do with him losing concentration? Rusty took Smithy's death harder than anyone. He kept tormenting himself that he could have got Smithy to slow down had he gone with him. Smithy was always speeding and had racked up a few fines in the last two years. He could be impulsive but usually listened to Rusty.

Rusty was the voice of reason in The Four Amigos. He lacked the confidence and good-natured banter of his three best mates but was still a key part of the group. He was usually the responsible one who organised getting them home safely and was the other mums' favourite. Girls did not see him as boyfriend material, like they did Smithy, but there were some who liked his shyness and ability to listen rather than talk.

When he left school, Rusty had briefly toyed with the idea of going away to study somewhere but he could not leave his mates behind. He had always been interested in electronics and how things like CCTV and intruder alarms worked. For the first time in his life, he showed some initiative. He went to see a few security companies about any jobs going and, to his delight, was offered a job. Rusty loved the work. He made a big impression on his boss, who took a liking to Rusty's attitude and work ethic. Some of the other young guys who had come and gone over the years had been unable to stick at the job for longer than a few months. Rusty was nearly three years into his time with the company and had been a fast learner.

When Smithy died, Rusty took some annual leave he had owing to deal with the grief and guilt he felt. His boss told him to have as much time as he needed. The first two weeks were the worst, but eventually he went back to work and could face people again. There was no problem doing his job but something deep down had changed. He felt like he needed a new challenge. Moving away was an option but he would give it time to see if that was really his best move.

Charlie Jennings was eyeing up another pint and his usual lunch of a mug of soup and a sandwich. You could say the jovial giant was a creature of habit. He liked to spend most lunchtimes in the bar before he walked home for an afternoon kip. Then it was back to the Beehive for another couple of pints to share the vibe with the locals dropping in after work. He had just turned 66, and the pub was his whole life.

Charlie had known The Four Amigos before they started drinking there. Andrew's dad—Ralph—and Charlie played rugby together at the North Shields Rugby Club. Charlie was a no-nonsense front row prop with the cauliflower ears to prove it, while Ralph had been the team's star player, scoring most of the points with his accurate goal kicking.

In those days, they drank at the Sportsman Pub but since Charlie had moved closer to the Beehive, he did not see much of Ralph anymore. He kept close tabs on his son and his friendly mates who always liked a chat. The boys didn't seem to mind when the old prop went off on one of his stories about the good old days of Whitley Bay. And there were lots of stories to tell.

Charlie loved his hometown. It saddened him how many talented young people had left to find their fortune elsewhere. He was not a big fan of the south and had only been to London once. He and Ralph had gone with their team for a weekend away to celebrate winning their Durham and Northumberland Two Division. Charlie got to see Buckingham Palace and Tower Bridge up close, which were the two landmarks he liked the most for some reason he could never put his finger on. Three of the boys were locked up for the night for touching up the strippers at a back street dive somewhere in East London but the rest of them made it home without any other drama.

Charlie understood why the bright lights of the big city seemed so appealing for young folk in North Shields and surrounding areas. He just thought that kids in their 20s like The Four Amigos should make a decision either way. If they want to go, then go. Otherwise, stay and make a difference.

'Make your minds up, boys. Either move on quickly somewhere else or stay here and make this a better place for everyone,' he liked to say.

It was just gone seven on a Thursday night when Charlie saw them arrive. Andrew was first and came over to say hi, followed by Joey and then Rusty. Any fool who knew them could see the sparkle had gone from their eyes and they lacked their usual banter. There was a sadness in the boys that broke Charlie's heart. He had always loved Smithy's jokes and stories of his latest romantic tryst.

'How are you coping, boys?' Charlie asked.

There was a general murmuring about getting there and taking it a day at a time before Rusty spoke with tears in his eyes.

'All I see is Smithy everywhere I go, and it hurts. I've been thinking about other options. I am worried I will be stuck here. What's the point? There must be better opportunities in Newcastle or I could get the overnight coach to London and see what I can find there. I feel a bit lost.'

'Yeah, that's a good idea. Not much for us here anymore,' Andrew added sadly.

Joey said nothing. He just looked down at the table and pulled a beer mat into tiny pieces.

Charlie waited till the conversation had come to an end. The old friends, broken by grief, were quietly drinking their beer and thinking about what they were going to do.

'I know it is not an easy time for you boys but please don't make any hasty decisions. You all have good jobs and I know you love this place. My dad used to call it the Blackpool of the North-East. When he was young, it was a favourite place for Glaswegians to come down from Scotland. That's how we ended up with Scottish blood in the family because he married a wee lass from Glasgow. One summer, he was kicking a ball around on the beach with a few mates when he spotted a pretty blonde sitting on the sand by herself.

'Back then he was a real ladies' man. Anyway, he chatted her up and they spent most of the two weeks she was here doing stuff together. They kept in touch and six months later, she moved to Whitley Bay. They were married for 40 years. They've both gone now—sadly.

'Well, boys, you know what I am going to say. I know it is a hard time for you but you need to make a decision with your lives. Either move on quickly somewhere else or stay here and make this a better place for everyone. I hope you decide to stay. Now, let me get a round in.'

Rusty was on his way home from having a couple of pints and a game of darts after work. It was six months after that pep talk from Charlie in the Beehive. The night was quite mild out, so he decided to walk along the Whitley Bay seafront promenade rather than get the bus. He liked the feeling of the fresh North Sea breeze blowing in his hair.

The abandoned buildings always made him think, no matter how many hundreds of times he had walked past them. The once-booming nightclubs and bars had mostly gone. Some of the old bed and breakfasts were used by the council for those who needed short-term accommodation. Rusty often thought about stuff like the unused buildings and the homeless when he was just walking and chilling. He was quite a deep thinker despite what people would imagine looking at him. Something about the combination of his unkempt red hair and unusually large ears led people, particularly teachers who should have known better, to think less of him. It was just the way it had always been but was a reason he never backed himself.

A loud, hacking cough coming from the concrete wall ahead of him startled Rusty from his thoughts. Propped up against the barrier was a sad-looking guy with a bushy beard, bloodshot eyes and a line of spit dribbling out the side of his mouth.

'Hey, my name is William. Have you got a spare quid so I can get a cup of tea please?'

Rusty often gave the standard reply of: 'Sorry, got no change,' because he was wary of getting too close to the homeless guys. A year ago, he had a nasty experience after being grabbed by one particularly aggressive character about a hundred metres from where he was now. It made him feel guilty to not help. This time he stopped. There was something about William's slightly posh accent and the polite way he had asked. Rusty fished around in his pocket and found a two-pound coin.

'Here you go. Do you mind telling me how you ended up homeless? You sound different from the other guys down here. I'm actually interested.'

William looked up and smiled, showing the gap where his front teeth used to take pride of place.

'Thanks. If you have got time, I am happy to tell you. It's not often I meet some random on the street who gives a damn.

Every homeless person has a different story. I had a privileged upbringing. My dad was a solicitor and we never lacked anything. I went to Durham Johnston Comprehensive School, then Durham University, where I got a good degree in history.

'My dad never forgave me for not following him into law. Instead, I went teaching. I started my first teaching position in Newcastle and it all went pear-shaped. First my mum died, and we were really close, then into the second year teaching, I started to suffer from severe anxiety and depression. I just fell apart. I was put on strong medication that had terrible side effects. So in desperation, I started taking a raft of drugs. I lost my job, fell in with a bad crowd at a rough pub near where I lived. I was drunk every day. I also took whatever drugs were going, as that was the only time I could escape my demons. Before I knew it, I was addicted.

'I came here one summer because I liked the beachfront and looking out to sea. It is very calming. I ended up living on the streets and have stayed ever since.'

Rusty took a few minutes to think about what William had said. It was the first time he had actually listened to someone who slept rough on the streets.

'Where do you stay, William? It must get cold here. Do you get help from anyone?'

'Yes and no. What's your name, son?'

'Rusty. Been called that ever since I was a kid. Red hair and all that. My real name is Michael.'

'Good for you, Rusty. Thanks. I like to sleep outside the shopfront because there is a little privacy and protection from the wind that can cut you in half. But the do-gooder council staff comes along sometimes and moves me on. Bastards. It happened earlier tonight. We get smashed twice if you think about it. The council wants us out of sight and out of mind while the government just doesn't give a shit. There are so many empty houses and properties along the waterfront. Did you see them back there? It's a disgrace. If the government cared enough, they would make money available for councils to turn some of those unused buildings into hostels for the homeless to live in. Every freezing winter here there are totally unnecessary deaths and none of those pricks in power could care less.

'The vast majority of us do not want to be living outside in all weathers, being pissed on and beaten up by drunks and lucky to have a hot shower once a month. We can go to the homeless shelter and get hot food and cups of tea, and there are plenty of good books to read. I go there every day and the people that run that place are absolute angels if you ask me.'

Rusty wished him luck and promised to look out for him and chat again. That night, as he tried to sleep, all he could think of was William's story. It took a long time to drop off but he woke determined to do something to help William and all the other poor souls like him.

A day later, Rusty dropped into the homeless shelter. Over a cup of tea, he learnt all about the great work they did for people like William. It did not take much convincing for Rusty to sign up to be a volunteer. He started helping out most weekends and loved catching up with William, who it turned out was a favourite among the staff. He was always so polite and had plenty of yarns to keep them all entertained.

A month after Rusty started volunteering, William came in with a big grin on his freshly shaven face. The beard was gone. He had washed his hair and was wearing clean clothes for the first time since he could remember.

'Hey, Rusty. Any biscuits going with a cuppa tea? I've got some good news. I finally got a hostel to stay in, and it could be long-term. Not sure about that but it is warm, safe and the people running it are good to deal with. Endless hot water. Bloody bliss, mate.'

'I'm so happy for you, William. You look great. I bet you feel like your life is restarting.'

'I do, and I am determined to get back my dignity, my self-confidence and to start again if I can. You never know I might even be able to work again and earn my own money.'

Rusty was delighted for William and, for the first time since Smithy died, happy within himself. It felt good. He went for his normal lunchtime walk past the Low Lights Tavern to the Fiddler's Green Fisherman's Memorial on the North Shields Quay. He loved the statue. It was his favourite place to sit and think, looking out to the North Sea.

Rusty was smiling. He knew what he was going to do with his life now. The idea to devote himself to working with homeless people like William had been brewing for a while. It was seeing what a completely changed man he was, with hope and sparkle back in his eyes, that convinced Rusty.

'I am going to make a bloody difference. Move on or stay and make a difference you say, Charlie. No doubts at all. I'm staying,' he said out loud to an unimpressed seagull.

Rusty laughed and kept walking. The day was just getting better.

*****

Seventeen Going Under

It was no surprise that Tom, Harry and I ended up as best mates. We were thrown together as terrified little 11-year-olds on Day One of our first year at Whitley Bay High School. We seemed to gravitate together as all nerds do, away from the good-looking kids, sports stars and bullies. We were all a bit chubby and were useless at sports – just cannon fodder for the school bullies who did not take long to start picking on us. Tom copped more than Harry and me because he was also a redhead and wore glasses. I know, he didn't get a lucky break there. You couldn't make it up.

But we all had to grin and bear it. There was little in the way of support from teachers and at its worst, when we were about 13 or 14, we never felt comfortable during breaks or before and after school. It was one of the reasons I was always angry at someone or about something but kept it all bottled up inside me. Who was there to talk to about stuff going down? I am 17 now and still have my moments, but hopefully I am through the worst of the pain I felt. But when you are in the middle of it all happening, it is just so hard to see a happy ending.

I was so angry with how my mum was treated by the Department for Work and Pensions. I thought they were supposed to help us but I never saw much sign of that. My mum was a nurse for 40 years. She spent 10 hours a day helping others, reducing fear and pain, always putting people at ease. For her dedication and selfless commitment, she was paid a pittance and had to put up with drunken idiots on night shifts at North Tyneside General Hospital's A & E department.

But that was nothing to what she had to deal with trying to get what she was entitled to at the DWP. Not many people knew my mum suffered from something called fibromyalgia. It is a condition where pain and stiffness is felt around your joints and in your muscles and bones. It can be triggered by physical or emotional stress, which she obviously had plenty of over the years.

Mum had widespread pain, fatigue and sleep disturbances. I came home from school one day and found her sobbing her heart out, saying she had to go to court to prove she was not fit to work. Her doctor had confirmed she could no longer work, that she had to rest and was definitely entitled to a disability allowance or similar weekly payment. Sadly, the DWP did not agree, so she had to endure the added stress of humbling herself in front of a judge, outlining all the symptoms she had and how they adversely affected her ability to work and pleading her case in tears.

I saw what that did to her. In the final judgement, she did get the allowance she was due and retired from her fulltime job at the hospital but it took ages for her to get better. I think she aged 10 years during that period with the court date hanging over her head plus having to work night shifts in so much pain. I was so angry and frustrated. How could the government treat my mum like this? She had worked hard all her life, never been in trouble with the law or missed paying a bill on time. I was old enough to understand what was going on, but unfortunately, I was not old enough to do anything about it.

I couldn't share my anger with anyone else. I loved Tom and Harry like brothers and we shared so many good times and laughs. We just didn't talk about what we felt or what worried us, apart from the night Tom was attacked on Whitley Bay Beach. One thing I did have was a great sense of humour. When all that anger was building inside me or I was being bullied, I tried to lighten the mood and use my natural humour as a way past it. When the sports jocks and teen studs were showing off and picking on Tom, Harry and me, I always had a quick one-liner to try and deflect the tension away. Sometimes it even worked.

At home, there was none of that. Mum's two friends would come round and have a glass of wine. The old girls always thought I needed cheering up. I didn't mean to be a miserable, little so-and-so at home. I just didn't feel like there was much to laugh about. Anyway, I despised mum's neurotic old friends, who drove me mad with their gossip and bollocks they talked.

Sometimes walking on Whitley Bay Beach could make my heart skip an extra beat. It is a beautiful place, especially as the sun is setting. In the summer, you can always see hundreds of people out and about on the beach, walking their dogs, playing football or just chilling out. It is only two miles from the big white dome on Spanish City, which everyone loves because of the cool vibe there, to St Mary's Island and the famous lighthouse. You have to walk across a concrete path to reach it but the problem is that you can only get across at low tide. I know plenty of guys who tried to do it drunk and tragically the odd one has drowned. They are idiots to try, if you ask me.

It was our favourite place until the night that Tom, Harry and I will never forget, even if we live to 90. We were all 14 at the time and had been hanging out around the beach most of the day. Not sure who it was, possibly me, but one of us decided it would be a good idea to go over to St Mary's Island and beat the tide to the lighthouse. It was just five minutes from where we were to get to St Mary's, so we had loads of time to get across and back, as high tide was an hour away.

We started walking towards the end of the beach, away from the concrete stairs leading down from the walkway below Spanish City, when three guys aged about 19 or 20 I had never seen before came up to us and asked if we had any cigs or dope.

'Who do you think we are then you idiots. Drug dealers?' I said, laughing out loud, trying to lighten the mood as usual. Not my finest moment.

Tom was closest to them and he laughed too. They turned from me with a look of anger in their eyes towards Tom. The biggest of the three grabbed him by the collar and threw him to the ground. The first kick was a shock, then the next landed and the next and the next. His mates just laughed while the big guy was putting the boot in. When they finally left, Tom was in a bad way. His nose was bleeding and he was making a soft groaning sound I had never heard before.

Harry and I just froze. We didn't know what to do. Then Harry rang 999 to get an ambulance. Some other people on the beach came over. Thankfully, one was a nurse who put

Tom in the recovery position and comforted him. Two policemen turned up quickly enough and asked a lot of questions, but they had no idea where the guys who attacked Tom had gone. It took 20 minutes for the ambulance to arrive. The paramedics took Tom away and told us to get hold of his parents. Harry made the call and we went home shocked and horrified. I mean, we knew shit like that went down all the time but we had never seen it. The roughing up we got at school was nothing like the beating Tom took. Just a few bruises, that's all. What they did to Tom was another league up altogether.

I went home and told Mum what had happened. She was so calm and managed to settle me down. I kept blaming myself for opening my big mouth and trying to be the funny guy as always. She told me not to be too hard on myself, as whatever I said did not deserve the treatment Tom got. We went to hospital a few hours later. Tom's injuries were bad enough to make him stay in overnight. He had a broken rib, superficial cuts and a concussion—oh, and broken glasses. Despite all that, he was in good spirits when we saw him. His parents were less pleased, bloody ropable to be honest, and demanding answers I didn't have about who had done this to their boy. I felt like I had let them down.

Tom recovered without any lingering scars you could see but he was never the same after the assault. He went out less than he used to and only went to the beach during the day. Tom never told his parents what I said. I love him for that but the guilt I felt just got worse and worse over time. Three years later, that night has never left me.

I replay that incident of Tom being kicked over and over again. I just froze and did nothing. If it happened again today,

I would defend Tom without thinking, no matter what happened to me. The fury I feel about what they did to Tom still festers with me. It just won't go away, making me even more bitter and twisted the longer time passes. I don't know to this day who those guys were. I have never seen them since. Harry says they were from South Shields, as his older brother knows some guys from there and heard a rumour about some kid getting beaten up on the beach. But what I can't understand is why Harry and I didn't do anything. We just stood there, frightened by the senseless violence. I know we were so young and small compared to those arseholes but we could have tried to stop it.

There were days after Tom got a kicking when I didn't think about it but not many. I'd dream about it at night and think about it every time we were back on Whitley Bay Beach. Little flashes of what happened would appear in my mind out of nowhere at any given time or place. And always I am there opening my gob, trying to be funny.

A year after Tom was attacked, I had my first crush on a girl. Suzie Shearer was the same year as us and the hottest girl in the class. Well, I thought so anyway. I never thought she would ever look twice at me. She went out with the class pin up—Marty Johnson, who was also the star striker for Whitley Bay Sporting Club, but I heard they had broken up because he was messing her around. My luck changed at the start of Term 3 as the summer started to heat up at last. We got put together along with three others to do a science project. It was the first time we had spoken to each other, and for some weird reason, she laughed at my jokes and impressions of teachers I liked to do. She and I went out on our own a few times. It was better than I could have hoped for. She kissed me the fourth time we went out. It was along the beach not far from where Tom got assaulted. For one of the few times, I was not thinking about what happened along that stretch of sand. I thought all my Christmases and birthdays had come at once.

I told Tom and Harry that it was the real thing. I asked my Mum what it felt like to be in love and if she thought I was in love. My head was all over the place but I had this giddy feeling whenever I saw Suzie or spoke to her at night, which we did all the time. Then *crash, bang!* Goodnight, nurse. She texted me one night to say she didn't want to go out with me anymore because she was getting back together with Marty. She said it had been fun but for me to move on.

I told Mum. She asked me if I was alright.

'Not really. I don't know what to think. Why did she text me? She could have talked to me face-to-face if she was going to drop me. It's not fair. I really liked her.'

That's when the tears welled up. I was ashamed, crying in front of my mother.

'It's just puppy love,' she said, giving me a hug. 'I know it seems like the end of the world right now and it may happen again. Sorry, you feel so hurt and sad but you will get over this quickly. Trust me.'

At school, there was one thing I liked. It was English. I loved reading, escaping whatever was going down at home or school and letting my imagination run wild. In my last year at school, I had Mr Sumner as my English teacher. We hit it off straight away and he was the first adult to really encourage me other than my mum.

My favourite place to escape to was the world of American author John Irving. I read *The Cider House Rules* first and still think of the main character—Homer Wells—as one of my mates. It's weird, I know, but when I have decisions to make or a problem I am struggling with, I just say to myself, 'Right, how would Homer deal with this?' It always seemed to help even if I didn't get it right.

But *Widow for One Year* is the book I love the most. Eddie O'Hare is my favourite character. We are both loners struggling to comprehend the world around us and how we fit in. Eddie was 16 in the first and best part of the book—the same age as me when I started reading it. He wanted to be a writer and, like me, had a liking for older women. Eddie had a passionate affair with 41-year-old Marion Cole that becomes a lifelong obsession while I had a thing for Tom's mum—Maggie. Tom never knew, and of course I never tried it on with her.

We live near Preston Cemetery. I know it is not everyone's cup of tea but I like to spend ages reading all the names on the graves, imagining who they were and what happened to them. The inscriptions on the tombstones are interesting. I guess I am thinking about potential characters for my future stories all the time without realising it. I started writing my own short stories this year. I'm not quite sure where they are going at times but trying to explain the chaos around me. Mr Sumner said not to worry about making them look pretty on the page but to let my imagination run wild.

'We can fix the spelling and grammar up later,' he'd say. He has given me some clues about what makes a good story work but has left me to it. He says I have loads of potential.

So instead of being directionless and not having any idea what I want to do, I now know. I want to be a writer, to create characters that make people laugh and cry. Just like my own life story really. Those feelings I had of misunderstanding what was going on, feeling angry all the time but not knowing why, and struggling to know what to do in the future, have now been banished to the past. With my writing goals, I have a different outlook on life. I finally know what I want to do. It won't be easy and there will be plenty of challenges along the journey, but I am determined to get there. I am applying for creative writing courses. Not sure if I will get in but I am trying hard. For the first time in my life, I am proud of who I am. That's a great feeling.

I am 17 and know exactly where I am headed.

f*****

Paradigms

Not many secondary school teachers can say they are universally liked by their students but then Rhys Mackie is no ordinary teacher. For so many of the teenagers he has taught during his 16 years in the job, he has been way more than just Mr Mackie, PE teacher. He has also been a father figure to them as sadly so many of the kids grow up without one.

Rhys has a simple philosophy when it comes to teaching. He treats everyone the same, no matter what their ethnic background or status, and he genuinely loves kids. Sounds simple and it is but it works for him. As a physical education teacher, Rhys has some advantages as most kids would rather be kicking a football, or sinking free throws on the basketball court, than sitting through another dreary science class. But it was the kids who were the most awkward and uncoordinated, the class geeks and those left to eat lunch alone, that loved his classes the most. In Mr Mackie they had one teacher they could talk to and ask advice without being made to feel like they were a nuisance or were wasting his time. They genuinely felt better for spending time with him.

And no teacher disliked bullying more than Rhys Mackie. He had been a sickly child growing up and had suffered some bullying by bigger, stronger kids. Only when he began to mature physically in his late teens, and his abundant sporting talents drew the right sort of attention, did he avoid any further repeat of that sort of treatment. But over the years he had never forgotten the fear, that sick feeling in his gut and the sleepless nights. Memories like that never leave you. He believed today's kids have it worse with social media being a constant harassment that sometimes never goes away. At least in his day, the bullying ended when he got home after the final bell of the day.

Bullying was something Rhys wished his teaching colleagues took more seriously. The amount of times he heard that "boys will be boys" from teachers who should know better, as some sort of pathetic justification for letting weaker kids be physically and mentally abused, made his blood boil. There have been plenty of times when he accused other teachers of being blinkered and having blood on their hands for allowing bullying to go on in and out of school. He was not the most popular person in the staff room because of that but he couldn't care less.

The tragic outcome of the "boys will be boys" mentality could be fatal. Rhys knew three boys who took their own lives after leaving behind social media posts describing the impact of bullying in heart-breaking, painful detail. He had taught them all. Two had been talented athletes who were making a name for themselves in cross country running. The last one to die was Ricky Bowyer two years ago. He was picked on for his liking for nail polish and his long hair but no one knew how much it had affected him. His last post explained when and where he was going to end it all but sadly no one saw it until too late. The next morning, a lady walking her energetic Jack Russell terrier on Tynemouth Longsands beach was alerted by the dog's frantic barking. Lying there was Ricky's body, washed up on the beach. He had just waded out to sea and kept going until the tide overcame him.

Rhys often thought of Ricky and what more he could have done to change what happened. He never saw any signs of abuse towards Ricky himself but wished he had asked more questions when he saw how unhappy the boy looked at times. It was one of many reasons why Rhys often struggled to enjoy a good night's sleep.

Rhys was better at running his classes and looking after his students than holding down a relationship. He was still single at 39 and did not have any kids himself. He often joked he had enough to look after every day at school. Rhys was popular with his friends and had female admirers over the years but lacked the confidence to do anything about it. Despite looking young for his age, and having what a female friend called a "kissable face", he suffered from self-esteem issues and avoided mirrors if he could. If he dug deep enough, he could probably place all his self-esteem issues squarely on the bullying he suffered. But deep thinking about his past was not something he enjoyed doing. He tended to dodge the subject of why he was still single. It mattered more to others than it did to Rhys. He actually enjoyed the solitary life.

The truth was Rhys had never got over being dumped by Helen Hunter. He had hoped they would get married and live happily ever after like in the soppy movies he had a weakness for. Rhys and Helen had been at school together but did not become an item until he was 25. They went out for nearly 12 months but the relationship ended rather abruptly when Helen decided to move to London where her parents lived. She told

Rhys she had a job to go to and did not want to be in a serious relationship anymore but Rhys often wondered what the real reason was. His efforts to keep in touch were mostly ignored so after a while he stopped trying. He was young, upset and bewildered. It took him ages to cope with being dumped and in the 14 years since Helen left he had never truly dealt with it.

Sure, he had other girlfriends over the years but nothing as serious as his relationship with Helen. She was his first serious love and he would have done anything for her. That nagging feeling there was unfinished business between them never really went away but he respected her need for privacy or whatever the reason was she blanked him. Sometimes, if he couldn't sleep, he went back over that old ground in his mind, trying to find a reason trapped in his subconscious somewhere that might spell out why she cut him off like she did.

Rhys would sometimes bump into Helen's overbearing sister Mary, who for some reason always made it obvious she had little time for him. His questions as to what Helen was doing and how she was keeping were always answered with a curt "she's fine, thanks" or "no change since I last saw you Rhys". It pissed him off, to be fair.

And then without warning, Helen came back into his life. It was the first day of term last September when he spotted her in the car park, two down from where he parked his car. She was with a student he had not seen before. She looked a little older around the eyes, and her hair was definitely a little greyer, but he could see her smile was still as dazzling as it always had been.

Rhys was just gawking at her with a startled look on his face when Helen saw him. There was an awkward moment as they looked at each other before Helen broke the silence.

"Rhys. How great to see you. I was hoping to bump into you. We haven't been back long from London. We moved here just a month ago. This is my son Jamie. He is starting school today. He just turned 14 and is in Year 9. Jamie, this is an old friend of mine Rhys Mackie. He teaches PE here."

Rhys thought the boy was her son alright. He had Helen's blue eyes and her cute dimples Rhys had always found adorable.

'Hey Helen. Great to see you. This is a nice surprise,' he managed to say, though his throat had suddenly got very dry. 'We must have a catch-up. Hi there Jamie. Welcome. I look forward to seeing you round the school. Do you play any sports?'

Jamie looked suspiciously from his mother to Rhys. He was a perceptive boy who understood his mother's moods better than anyone. There was definitely some sort of nervous tension or something weird between them. He was not expecting the first teacher he would meet to be an old friend of his mother and something of a mystery at that.

'Hi Sir. I like most sports,' Jamie replied. 'Rugby and athletics are my favourites. I like cross country running best of all.'

'Excellent. They are my passions too,' Rhys said, managing a smile. 'When I was your age I loved long distance running and kicking goals for fun playing rugby. Would you like me to show you to your form class?'

'Thanks Sir, that would be great.'

34

Helen wished Jamie well for his first day and thanked Rhys for helping out. She promised to get in touch, maybe go and have a drink sometime.

Rhys watched her leave. Jamie could see by the way he was watching his mum leave that there was history between them alright. 'This is going to be interesting,' he thought to himself.

Rhys and Jamie crossed paths often throughout the school year. Jamie was not in his class but Rhys coached his rugby team and the cross country runners, so he got to know the polite, quiet kid very well. Jamie was a natural goal kicker with his left foot just like Rhys had been. They also shared the same loping stride which was typical of long distance runners. Jamie trained hard but lacked the stamina and speed to reach any great heights. Sadly, school turned out to be somewhat of an ordeal for Jamie, apart from the sports he loved. A friend he made in the rugby team told Rhys that Jamie was getting a hard time from some guys in the year ahead who liked to intimidate new boys to the school.

Jamie was reluctant to discuss it. He told Rhys it was not a big deal.

'Jamie, promise me you will come and see me immediately if there is anything you can't handle or they hurt you. Promise me?' asked Rhys when he talked to Jamie about it.

'Yes Sir. Don't worry. I dealt with worse than them when I was at school in London.'

A week later, Rhys was sitting at his desk in the sports office at the school gym when he heard the unmistakable sound of a beating going on in the boys' toilets. The distinctive thud of fists and kicks landing and the grunts of the victim left nothing to the imagination.

Rhys sprinted down the corridor and burst into the toilet. Two bigger boys were laying into a third smaller kid cowering on the floor in the corner. Another boy he recognised immediately as Simon McCormack was filming the whole thing on his phone. Rhys grabbed the two thugs putting the boot in and swung them round to face him. He taught them both and knew them well.

'Hampton and Garratt, I am surprised at you two. You should know better than beating up another student. You disgust me. Go and wait in my office. You too McCormack. Go now."

They trudged off out the door. Rhys could see for the first time who was on the floor, with blood dripping from his nose. It was Jamie.

'Oh no, Jamie. What the hell has happened here? Are you okay?'

'Yes Mr Mackie. I'll be fine. My ribs hurt and I think my nose is a bit of a mess. Thanks for stopping them.'

'Look, let's get you up. I want you to go see the nurse to get checked over.'

Jamie got to his feet. He was a bit dizzy but after he washed his face he felt better. The blood had washed away and thankfully there were just a few bruises. He would have a black eye for a week or so but no lasting physical damage.

'Why did they attack you Jamie?' Rhys asked with tears welling in his eyes.

'They often hassle me for money or try to steal my phone, Sir. I don't take any crap from them and they don't like me standing up to them. Today is the first time they have hit me like this. Thanks again Mr Mackie. You are always there for me. I'll go now and see the nurse. I just wish it would stop. I'm always looking over my shoulder to see if they are around. Nobody should be scared like this.'

Rhys always prided himself on his even temperament, even under the most extreme duress that a class of rebellious teenagers can impose. But faced with the students who had beaten up Jamie was more than he could bear. For once, he lost his temper and raised his voice to such an extent that the gymnastics class in the gym stopped the exercises they were doing to listen to what was going on.

'What gives you thugs the right to physically attack another student like that? Have you any idea what damage you have done both physically and mentally? What has he ever done to you?' Rhys yelled at the three bullies.

'That boy wouldn't hurt a fly. How would you feel if I started laying into you like that? I am so disappointed in you three. I know what your parents will think when I tell them.'

While Hampton and Garratt looked suitably chastised, McCormack let a slight smirk crease his face that Rhys spotted.

'You think this is funny McCormack? Right, you disgust me the lot of you. We are off to the headmaster's office and I will be pushing for you all to be expelled. Not so funny now, McCormack.'

Rhys and the boys filed into headmaster Rob Young's office. He was a known disciplinarian with a long-held goal to eradicate racism and bullying from his school. A month earlier, he sent out an email to all staff outlining why bullying was so dangerous and had to be stamped out.

'Bullying creates a cycle of harmful, repeat behaviour. What I mean is, if bullying is not dealt with at the time, at school, it can lead to feelings of deep anxiety and incredibly low self-esteem in adulthood. In some cases, it can lead to suicidal thoughts and students taking their own lives. Sadly, we have all had to deal with the trauma afterwards from that. It can also be incredibly disruptive for families, especially if other family members don't know it is happening or don't fully understand what is going on.'

Rhys told Rob what happened at the gym and the condition Jamie was in. Rob thanked him for bringing the students to him and said he would deal with them. Rhys went back to his office. On the walk back to the gym he could not get that final comment Jamie had said out of his mind.

'Nobody should be scared like that.'

It struck a chord. Rhys had seen the impact of bullying over many years of teaching. He had stopped it immediately if it happened on his watch but apart from hauling out other teachers from time to time, he knew he could have done more over the years so there was an element of guilt in his thinking.

Later that night he tried to come up with some ideas about how to raise awareness around school bullying. It was not easy for him as he mostly let others do the talking at staff meetings and drive new ideas. Rhys liked to have a shot or two of whisky after dinner but he ended up having three extra glasses. The whisky added to his depressed mood and brought tears to his eyes again as he remembered the kids who had paid the ultimate price from being bullied. Thoughts of Ricky always made him well up.

The extra drams made Rhys get up during the night and go to the toilet. On his way back to his bedroom he saw his old Beatles T-shirt on the floor. He remembered how cool it was that so many thousands of fans had worn something similar to the Paul McCartney concert he went to a few years ago. He still loved that shirt and people sometimes asked him about it. It had the famous *Abbey Road* album cover on the front.

'T-shirts,' he thought to himself. They could be the answer to the puzzle he had been trying to solve all night. Kids love wearing tees and with the summer in full heat, now was the time to get some made. 'We could sell them and use the money to raise awareness for mental health issues like bullying,' he said aloud. Rhys went back to bed and slept soundly. Next morning at school he went to see the art teacher he got on well with. John Sanders was a decent guy who always looked out for his students. Once Rhys explained what he wanted to do, John immediately was keen to run with the project.

'Leave it with me, Rhys. I will get my senior class this morning to come up with a cool design for the T-shirts. This is a great idea.'

What they came up with was a vibrant coloured shirt with a clear message - *NOBODY SHOULD BE SCARED. STOP BULLYING IN SCHOOLS.*

Rob Young agreed to fund the shirts and the giant banners that were put up around the school.

'There is always money to siphon off from the school board's entertainment budget,' he told Rhys, laughing.

Rob also agreed with an idea Rhys had to put the three students who beat up Jamie on playground duty selling the T-shirts every day for a month. It was either that or face suspension. They were reluctant at first to do it but faced with the alternative they had no choice, so decided to make the best of it. The first week they sold 20 shirts at five pounds each, then 40 the next week, 75 the third week and 90 the final week. The school community got right behind the campaign and a committee was formed, chaired by Rhys, to decide on the best awareness campaigns they could put together with the large amount of money they now had.

To be fair, the three bullies who sold the T-shirts had shown plenty of remorse for their actions. They each emailed Jamie an apology, which his mother appreciated more. Jamie regarded Rhys as the hero in this whole episode and he took every opportunity to tell his mother what a great guy Mr Mackie was. Helen was grateful how Rhys had looked after her son. They had seen each other quite often over the winter at Jamie's rugby games and seemed more comfortable in each other's company. She was settling back into life in North Shields and had a job as a senior accountant that kept her busy with long hours. There did not appear to be any man in her life but as usual Rhys was slow to do anything about it.

Rhys had one lingering, unanswered question. Who was Jamie's father? Considering how Jamie's age matched nicely with when Helen left town, it did cause Rhys to wonder if he was Jamie's father. Sometimes, when Jamie was not looking, Rhys would stare at the boy intently, looking for any tell-tale marker that might point to him being his dad. Rhys had asked Jamie about his father but did not get much back. It seems his father was not around for his birth and his mother did not try to contact him. Jamie had never met his dad.

When Helen finally invited Rhys round to her house for dinner, to thank him for looking out for Jamie after the assault, the subject of who his father was came up easier than Rhys imagined it would. Dinner had gone well and it was just Helen and Rhys sitting in the lounge after Jamie went to his room. Helen seemed more relaxed than Rhys had seen her for years, no doubt helped by drinking the best part of a bottle of chardonnay.

'Rhys, I have a secret to tell you. I really am sorry for not being honest about why I left all those years ago and I should have been. The truth is that I was having an affair with someone when we were going out together. He was going to leave his wife, and he wanted me to leave you, but then I got pregnant.

'I had a test and it proved it was his, not yours. I was really struggling and had a partial nervous breakdown or something like that. Remember those anxiety attacks I used to get towards the end? Well they were part of my mental health issues. I had to get out of town and go to my mum's. I don't know what I would have done without her. I know it was cruel of me to not tell you what was going on but I just couldn't. I didn't tell Jamie's father for a while either. When I did contact him six months after Jamie was born, he wanted nothing to do with either of us. Since then I have not spoken to him once. Last I heard he moved to Glasgow about 10 years ago.'

Rhys was about to say something but changed his mind. He looked at Helen with a pensive look on his face. She knew him well enough to wait. He always used to take his time sorting through problems and difficult topics.

'Well thanks for telling me finally, Helen. It means a lot. It answers a few of the questions I have struggled with for years. So who did you have the affair with, the guy who is Jamie's dad?'

'Look Rhys, it won't help for you to know. He was an older guy I worked with and we only were seeing each other for three months. I don't think you knew him."

Rhys and Helen talked for two more hours. All the gaps from the missing years were filled in. They realised they still had so much in common. Jamie was another unifying part of the puzzle they were putting back together after all those years apart.

Around midnight, Rhys got up to leave.

'Thanks Helen. This has been the best night I have had since, well, you know when. You have no idea how happy you have made me feel. I'd like to do it again soon, if that's okay with you.'

'Oh, it's more than okay with me, Rhys. I have missed you so much. Could we start again?'

*****

Spit of You

There is no way to test if your nan is better than all the others but I know I got lucky with mine. When I was just a little kid, I used to tell her I could see a light shining off her forehead that no one else could see. It became our private little secret we shared, our own special bond if you like.

Sometimes she would look at me and ask if the light was still shining. It made us laugh and that was something that was in short supply at times in our house.

Nan was my dad's mum and lived with us. One of my earliest memories is sitting up on one of the stools we had in the kitchen, watching nan bake her famous singing hinnies. I must have been about four, I guess.

Her yummy scones always tasted better than any others I tried.

'The secret is to make sure the butter is really cold and don't be tight with the currents,' she used to say. 'The more fruit, the better the flavour.'

Nan was my private sounding board. At home, she was the one I spent the most time with. She always had time for me and listened to me if I needed to let go of whatever was bugging me. She loved talking about the old days when she was a girl growing up near Newcastle. Money was in short supply back then but they had plenty of fun. She was happily married for 19 years until her husband was killed by a drunk driver.

All the stories about her beloved Harry were about good times and happiness. I wish I had known him. He would have been easier to live with than my dad, and I think we would have got on well. I struggled to understand Dad when I was younger but we were more alike than I realised. We have the same eyes and square jaw, same stubborn attitude and short fuse, taking out our frustrations on whatever was closest.

I have so many memories of waking up to the sound of raised voices, followed by all sorts smashing in the kitchen. It used to scare the shit out of me but I never made a fuss. We were not that sort of a family.

I tried talking to my mum about it but she just told me not to worry.

'It's just your dad letting off some steam,' she'd say.

Mum used to clean the mess up. She was so stoic, so practical about it all. Nothing seemed to phase her. I'd get up the next morning and there was nothing out of place, no sign that cups and glasses had ended up smashed to bits. If there was a positive to come out of all the drama, it was that Dad never once hit Mum, which was just as well. I don't think I could ever have forgiven him if he had.

My dad Alan, or Big Al as his mates called him, was a born-and-bred Tynesider. His generation of hard grafters didn't talk about feelings or mental health issues. They buried whatever their problems were deep inside. The pain only came out when they had drunk too many pints. Newcastle Brown Ale was my dad's tipple of choice and he drank plenty of it. That's just our way of dealing with things where we live.

I never had any trouble talking to other kids, my teachers or adults I met, but I always struggled to talk to my dad about stuff that mattered to me. Any time I tried, he just clammed up. It was mostly me being scared of something or occasionally being bullied at school—just the usual things boys worry about. I often wondered if his own dad's tragic death was the thing he never got over. My nan hinted at it a few times but what was eating my dad up was one of the few things she did not talk to me about. It was just too hard, I guess.

It was sad he found it impossible to communicate with Mum or Nan about the anger he felt inside. In the end, it was his increasingly erratic behaviour and heavy drinking that caused my dear old mum to finally tell him to go. She just couldn't deal with it anymore. Dad left when I was 12. At first, I thought I could handle it but I started to get unexplained pains in my chest. I went to the doctor and had loads of blood tests done but everything came back fine. After a few months, the pain went away but sometimes if I got stressed about school or thought about my dad, it came back again for a while.

Dad had a great mate Barry Wilder, who was making good money and having the time of his life working on a big engineering project in New Zealand. Barry asked Dad to join him, as there was plenty of work going. It was too good an opportunity to let pass, so he decided to go and make a new start. It was about as far away from me he could go in the world. I looked it up on the internet. Auckland is 11,178 miles away from Newcastle, so that means 11,186 miles from North Shields. It is so far away that the time in Auckland is 11 to 12 hours ahead of us, depending on daylight saving times. Bloody hell!

Dad came round to the house one morning to say goodbye. I was sad he was leaving us to go so far away but also pleased for him. It sounded like a great adventure and it was the happiest I had seen him in ages. My mum looked happy too. She could see his old sparkle was back. Just for an hour or so before he left, he was the man she fell in love with all those years earlier. Mum was also hopeful of getting some decent child maintenance money from him that too often he had spent down at the local pub.

It turns out my nan was the one who encouraged him to go. She could see the chance of a lifetime was there for the taking. As Dad was leaving, she kissed him on the cheek.

'This is a great opportunity, son. You will always regret it if you stay here and don't try your luck. I think it will be the making of you. Don't stuff it up, mind.'

Despite the difficulties we faced, there was lots of good times my dad and I shared. Dad was great with his hands. He was an electrician and specialised in refrigerated units, servicing the large fishing fleet based out of North Shields and the wider North-East area. He taught me all the basic stuff to do with wiring and fixing all that can go wrong with the electrics. I loved hanging out with him tinkering around fuse boxes and learning new things.

We both were passionate Newcastle United fans and once or twice a season, he would take me to St James' Park. He worked most weekends and was on call a lot of the time, so we never had season tickets, but he could always call in a favour to get match-day tickets. I bloody loved every minute.

Dad didn't like talking about his feelings with me, or "soppy shit" as he called it, but he loved to have a laugh with his mates. If there was any banter going down, he was likely to be in the middle of it. People gravitated to Dad in a positive way. When we had parties round ours, it was his voice cracking the jokes I could hear in bed. He always got the most laughs when he was drunk. Later on, it was something I realised came naturally to me as well. It was easy to make people laugh and sometimes even my teachers let me off if I deserved a detention. They appreciated having a laugh more than anyone—the poor sods.

I got my first girlfriend when I was 15. Barbara McKenzie was her name and she was probably my best friend too. We met on my first day as a shy, little five-year-old in Year 1 at King Edward Primary School. The class teacher, Mrs Thomas, paired me up with Barbara so she could show me the ropes and look after me. Barbara had been at school for six months, so knew everything I had to know. Come to think of it, when we started going out together, she knew more about lots of other stuff than I did. I guess she was always one step ahead of me.

I am not likely to ever forget my 16th birthday. It was a beautiful, warm spring morning, tempting us that summer might not be too far away. I met up with Barbara. We biked across to Whitley Bay Beach, which was one of our favourite places. It was just perfect. Walking along the beach, talking about whatever was on our minds, eating fish and chips for lunch from Fisherman's Bay and collecting shells for my nan. She loved to get fresh shells to add to the little bowls she put around the house.

'Just to remind me of the sea, you know, pet,' she would say.

I got back home just after three in the afternoon. One look at my mum's face told me something terrible had happened.

'It's your nan, love. Her heart just stopped or something. I called her for lunch and when she didn't come, I looked in her room. She was lying on the bed. Not moving, not breathing. The ambulance came but it was too late. She had already passed away. I'm so sorry, son.'

Have you ever had a moment where time and everything just seems to stop? You are there but not there, like you are staring into your own dream. It was like that for me when Mum told me the news. The rest of that day was a trial to endure in slow motion as I tried to deal with what had happened. At least my dad was there. I needed him, and even though he didn't say much, it was great comfort to have him home.

Dad had come back from New Zealand a few months earlier but was not living with us. He made plenty of money out there and had good future prospects, until his fists took over one night on the booze after a disagreement with his boss about pay rates. Punching out the one guy giving you work and allowing you to stay in the country was not Big Al's greatest moment. So he came home with his tail between his legs but I didn't care about that.

I kept telling myself, 'I won't cry in front of Dad,' but I couldn't help it. He just looked into space. He didn't cry or comfort me or anything. He was doing it tough, my mum said, and I knew how he felt. The night before Nan's funeral, I was trying to sleep but couldn't stop thinking of her. All those special times we had spent together and how the light shining from her never went out. There are so many things I always meant to ask her but never did. You always think there is plenty of time and you will get round to it one day. But you never do. All the answers from the past are now locked away forever behind a sealed door, and that hurts.

The day of the funeral was cold and wet, as it often is in September. Mum said the rain was God's tears falling for Nan. I liked that. She made me wear my second-hand suit, which was fine, as I wanted to look my best. Dad looked smart too but had a weird look on his face. I couldn't work out what it meant but he didn't say a word. A good number of people turned up at the little chapel. Nan was in an open coffin, so we could all see her face. She looked so still and serene, so utterly at peace. I thought it would freak me out to see her lying there but it actually helped me accept she was gone.

A few family friends got up and said nice things about Nan. My dad was last.

Quietly, in a whispered voice that sounded more like a boy than my dad, he spoke from the heart for the first time I could remember.

'I'm sorry, Mum. I should have been there for you and listened more. I should have helped out more. Please forgive me. You did everything for me when I was growing up and I never thanked you for it. I was lucky to have you on my side. All those chances I was given to make a success of my life, I just threw away. I let you down but you never gave up on me. You were my rock. Thank you for everything. You were one in a million.'

Dad was standing by Nan's coffin, just staring at her, not moving. He was so big and strong, but for the first time he looked so fragile to me. The chapel was silent. You could almost hear your own breathing, and a few people cleared their throats and stifled coughs.

Dad's lips started to quiver. He closed his eyes and tried to hold back the tears but it was too late. They ran down his cheeks and his big frame shook with sobs. I had never seen my dad cry, never seen him show any sort of emotion if I come to think of it. In that moment, his pain really hit me hard. I felt so much love for him. He sat down next to me. I gave him a look that said, 'I'm with you, Dad.' He nodded back and touched my arm. It was a special moment between us.

I don't know why but I suddenly thought of the future. There will come a time, hopefully a long way off, when it will be my dad lying there in a coffin and me standing over him.

I looked over at Nan.

The reflection from the church lights was shining on her forehead, just like I always imagined it when I was a kid. Our special bond.

*****

Will We Talk

Johnny Henderson never expected much out of life. His parents did not have any money to spend on extras. Just paying for rent, food and all the other bills that seemed to stack up was a challenge. But they were a content little unit, with plenty of good-natured chatter making for a happy house. Johnny and his mum were always close, even during the tumultuous teenage years. His dad was not a great drinker and worked hard as a brickie on building sites across the North-East.

Johnny went to Norham High School. He was a good student, kept out of trouble and passed most of his exams. He knew if he wanted to reach his goal of being a professional footballer, he had to first do well at school. He was goal-driven from as long as he could remember. His football skills were miles ahead of his peer group, right from the age of seven when he first started to make a name for himself with North Shields Football Club, located close by the school. Johnny could dribble with ease around and through defenders of all sizes and shoot powerfully with both feet. He was the star player, no doubts.

Like every football kid growing up in North Shields, Johnny wanted to one day pull on the famous black and white stripes of Newcastle United. That day came earlier than he could have imagined when just after his 16th birthday, his dad got a call from the head coach of the club's Football and Education Development Programme. Johnny was offered a place to train and play for Newcastle United Foundation in the National Football Youth League and Cup. He got to wear the official Newcastle kit, which gave him a special thrill every time he put it on. The educational part of the programme meant Johnny was supported to gain a Level 2 Certificate in Sport through Newcastle College. It was the best of both worlds.

There were plenty of nerves meeting the other boys and the coaches for the first time but he soon fit in. Johnny quickly impressed them all with his talent on the training pitch, plus his dedication to his studies was another good sign. He often dreamt of scoring the winning goal at St James' Park against Liverpool in the Premier League. That was the team he wanted to beat the most, as his dad was from there originally and supported the reds. It created plenty of good banter at home growing up.

Johnny had a few starts and appearances off the bench in his first season in the academy but his second campaign was where he grew up, on and off the pitch. He played in 14 of the 19 games leading up to the season finale against Everton, the blue team from Liverpool, at Wallsend Boys Club in Newcastle. He had scored the winning goals against Liverpool and Burnley and was keen to finish the season in style. He probably should have scored in the first half when he hit the post from a close range header before his world collapsed from under him.

It happened out of nothing. As he chased a ball into the penalty area, Johnny collided at speed with an opponent. The impact caused a double compound fracture of his right shin. It was a horrific injury that not only finished his season but his career. Surgeons were able to save his leg after a serious infection following the operation, but it was a close-run thing. Weeks of rehab stretched out to months. Anyone close to Johnny could see his confidence and will to carry on fading away. But thanks to his close family and mates, particularly Paul Wood, he made it through the other side with some of his sense of humour still in place.

The stunning Cullercoats promenade was where he began to heal mentally. During the warmer spring and summer months, he liked to park up on one of the large seats primed for the best views across the North Sea. If he was on his own, he focused on the view and tried not to think about what happened to him, what might have been as a footballer and what the future held. Shifting his mind into neutral was advice he got from a trainer at Newcastle, and it really helped. The best times were when Woody came with him. Johnny could talk things through with him that he couldn't do at home or to the counsellor he was working with. Sometimes they just talked crap and watched the girls go by. Those hours sat looking out to sea really helped Johnny blow the dark clouds away. Woody had more common sense than anyone he knew and was a good listener. In the months that followed the injury, Johnny had plenty to get off his chest.

A year later, Johnny passed his Level 2 qualification and started on his Level 3 diploma. He could walk without much of a limp but running hurt, so he gave it away. He started hitting the pubs and fast food replaced the athlete's diet he had stuck to so religiously. You couldn't blame him after what he had been through, but Woody was worried. His mate was putting on too much weight and getting into the odd scrap when his mouth started to run away after his fifth or sixth pint.

Johnny's 19th birthday was coming up on Saturday night. Woody organised a few of the old school gang and the two guys from Newcastle United that Johnny was closest to for a boys' night out at the Low Lights Tavern. It was Johnny's favourite pub and next to the Fish Quay where he bought the fresh seafood his dad loved so much.

They were all looking forward to a great night.

Chrissie Taylor always had plenty to say. She had strong opinions on how women were portrayed in the media and how poorly treated they were regarding equal pay against their male counterparts. She would happily accept being labelled a feminist.

She was also staunchly left-wing and wanted the UK to become a fairer society. During Covid-19 lockdowns, she immersed herself in learning as much as she could about the political landscape and how each party fit into the puzzle. Her research left her no closer to an answer.

Her parents had always voted Labour but Chrissie was not impressed with any of the major parties. She was cynical about all the leaders and their motivation for being in politics. She struggled to keep her cool whenever Boris Johnson made an appearance on the news. Something about the way he never combed his hair or did his tie up properly really got to her.

You could say she had unconventional good looks with a slightly crooked nose and a beautiful smile, but she hated people being defined by looks or wealth. To win her trust and heart, you had to have core values that equated with hers and most importantly show everyone the same respect. Most boys didn't stand a chance with her. She was never impressed by random chat up lines or who was the best footballer. There were one or two boys that she didn't mind. They shared the same classes at Marden High School, most notably Mike Dawson and Dean Barker, but her best friends Sarah Smith and Jo Allan were her mainstays.

The trio did pretty much everything together. They loved watching movies at the Odeon Silverlink Cinema, particularly big-budget romantic films or a horror flick. None of them was into sports, so from when they first met aged 13, they loved to just hang out together during breaks and after school. They all lived within a few blocks of each other not far from Tynemouth Pier Lighthouse, on the point between the North Sea and the River Tyne. That was where they liked to go for long walks and hang out when the weather was good. The pier extends 900 metres out to sea, and if they timed it right, they could be at the end when ferries or cruise ships came through the gap with South Shields Lighthouse. It was an awesome sight.

Chrissie loved history and drama above everything else she studied. Every year, the school staged a large production and Chrissie made it her personal crusade to get a major role if she could. She could really act and was a great dancer but the thing that held her back was her alto singing voice, the lowest in the female voice range. Still, in the last four years at school, she had key roles in *Bugsy Malone*, *We Will Rock You*, *The Addams Family* and *Grease*, which was a major achievement.

The undoubted highlight was playing Betty Rizzo in *Grease*. Chrissie just loved the character, which is tough, sarcastic and outspoken but also shows her vulnerable side when she had a pregnancy scare. By the end of the show's run, she had more in common with Betty Rizzo than Chrissie would have ever wanted. It was during intensive weeks of rehearsals that she and Mike went from friends to going out together. It was Chrissie's first serious relationship. Mike played Kenickie Murdoch, Betty's boyfriend, so there was plenty of close action and kissing between the two budding young actors. They had played romantic leads before, but this time, there was a spark neither knew existed before.

Chrissie was initially reluctant to take the relationship past movies, McDonalds and walking along the pier, but after a few weeks, she realised she really liked Mike. He was the perfect boyfriend, or so she thought. He had nice manners, always looked good, was from a popular family and did not put any pressure on Chrissie for sex. But she wanted to do it with him. Sarah and Jo had boyfriends, so Chrissy decided it was time. Mike organised it for when his parents were out. He had more experience than she had, and she trusted him. Chrissy was nervous as hell but eventually relaxed and enjoyed it. It was not too uncomfortable. Certainly way better than some of the stories she had heard from other girls at school, including Jo, who found losing her virginity a nightmare.

In the weeks that followed, Mike was attentive and generous, buying her gifts and talking about what they might do after they left school. They had sex a few more times with Mike using a condom every time, but when Chrissie's period was late, she panicked.

'No, no, no, no, this can't be happening,' she wailed to herself in her bedroom.

Luckily, it was a false alarm, as she was just 10 days late. Thank God for that because a week later, Chrissie's perfect Prince Charming broke her heart. It was just a few days after *Grease* finished. The call came on a Monday at about 11 p.m. Chrissie was nearly asleep and was startled by her mobile ringing. It was another friend, Jess Marshall, who played Frenchy in *Grease*.

'Hey. What's up, Jess?'

'Hi, Chrissie. I'm sorry to have to tell you this but I can't keep it to myself anymore. I have too much respect for you and I hate cheating dogs. Mike has been having it off with Sally for about a month. You deserve better.'

Chrissie couldn't take it in at first. Sally had played the main female lead Sandy Olsson in *Grease*. Chrissie believed Jess as they had known each other since they were nine and shared similar values. She did not sleep much that night and felt numb the next morning. Her Mum asked her if she was okay.

'No, I'm feeling sick, Mum. I think I might not go to school today.'

She went back to bed. First call she made was to Mike.

'Is it true then, you and Sally?'

His long pause before he answered was like a kick in the guts. She had hoped in her heart Jess was wrong and that Mike could explain it away.

'I'm sorry, Chrissie. It just happened one night. Never planned it, never wanted to hurt you. You know I love you. Let's sort this out.'

'Like hell, Mike! I never want to see you ever again. All that stuff about loving me and wanting to do stuff together next year was just bullshit. I hate you.'

And that was that.

After school finished, there was only one thing Chrissie wanted to do—go to drama school and kick-start an acting career. She had gained valuable experience with ACT 2 CAM after-school drama classes in Whitley Bay before being accepted for the prestigious Project A actor-training company in Newcastle.

She had only just heard the good news and was set to start the course in a month. Sarah suggested they all go out Saturday night to a few bars to celebrate Chrissie's brilliant news, starting at the Low Lights. They often went there for a few drinks and to eat. Jumbo-battered king prawns with chips were Sarah's favourites, while Chrissie and Jo were partial to the tasty homemade pies. There was a vibe in the place they loved and the history, of course.

'It dates back to 1657 and is the oldest pub in North Shields,' history-buff Chrissie happily told anyone who asked.

She always got a smile and a chat from the cheeky barman she quietly had a crush on. She would never have the guts to flirt with him, or God forbid ask him out for a drink, but he was definitely her favourite. She hadn't had a boyfriend since Mike, so was in no rush.

The barman was something of a musician as well. When it was quiet, he loved to slip from behind the bar, grab his guitar and belt out a couple of tunes. Chrissie thought he was pretty good too.

Johnny and Woody arrived at Low Lights just before 7 p.m. The place was busy and loud, with loads of Newcastle fans celebrating that afternoon's 2-1 win over West Ham. The other boys were already there, two pints ahead of them at a table close to the bar. They greeted Johnny and Woody warmly.

'This is going to be a great night, mate. Happy birthday, Johnny,' Woody whispered in his ear, heading to the bar.

It did not take long before they had two pints down them and that early buzz you get from the first couple of drinks. Then it becomes a gradual slide into getting drunk, which these days took Johnny a bit longer than it used to. It was his round, so he went over to the bar and started talking to the manager about football. He was feeling happier than he had for a long time.

Chrissie, Sarah and Jo arrived about 8:30 p.m. It took them ages to get an Uber, which was a pain but they quickly forgot about it when they walked in. The place was heaving, with lots of familiar faces from school and work plus the Newcastle fans in good form.

Chrissie noticed that her favourite barman was not working. Never mind. She ordered a round of drinks—white wine for her and Sarah, half of Guinness for Jo—and turned to see a nice-looking guy with sad eyes waiting for his drinks next to her. There was something about him that grabbed her attention. Maybe it was that thousand-yard stare or something.

'Penny for them,' Chrissie said, realising too late it was what her mother always said when she was a kid.

He looked up, half-startled and half-amused.

'Sorry, I was miles away. How are you doing? You just arrived?'

'Yeah. I'm with a couple of friends. Busy tonight, eh? I love it when it's like this. I'm Chrissie, by the way.'

'Johnny. Nice to meet you,' he said, smiling at her. 'I better take these drinks back to the boys. Have a good night. Let's have a drink later.'

There was some eye contact and smiles between them over the next two hours. They did get to talk for a while when ordering drinks again. Johnny told her it was his birthday, so she kissed him on the cheek. That felt good.

Johnny finally went over to Chrissie around 11. He was pissed but thought he was still making sense, so it was now or never.

'Hey, Chrissie. I'd like to get to know you. I don't want to be too cocky but how about come back to mine for a drink and see what happens?'

She was surprised he asked but pleased too. There was something about this guy that intrigued her. Yes, he was a bit drunk but she was sick of being the good, boring girl who went home alone. It was her time to have some fun and he seemed much nicer than others she had met recently.

Chrissie was not a fan of one-night stands. She hated how women were judged so badly, yet men were applauded. What she said to Johnny came out a little too rapid fire but she wanted to make sure he understood her values.

'Look, Johnny. I want you to know I haven't been with a guy for ages and am usually pretty slow coming forward, to be fair. It is important to me that you don't just think I am another one-night stand. I really would like to get to know you.'

He smiled at how serious she looked and all the questions.

'Of course. I really do want to get to know you better too. I think you are pretty and nothing changes if you say yes or no. Let's get out of here.'

They said their goodbyes and left. Outside, two guys were throwing harmless drunken punches at each other with their girlfriends yelling at them to stop. Johnny and Chrissie laughed at the scene and walked away, holding hands and smiling. He lived 15 minutes away by taxi, not too far from Chrissie's place as it happened. He kissed her softly on the lips. She smiled and returned the kiss with more passion. She hadn't felt like this for ages. What Mike did to her a year ago still really hurt but she knew she had to move on and start trusting men again.

Johnny's place was in a good street and cleaner than she expected. He took some white wine out of the fridge and poured two large glasses. They sat together on the couch. She realised he really was drunk. He was slurring his words and told Chrissie he just wanted a nice girl like her as he got so lonely since he broke his leg.

'What do you mean broke your leg? What happened, Johnny?'

'Long bloody story, darling. It ruined my life and I just can't get over it. Sorry, but that's just the way it is. I don't know if I will ever get over it.'

He looked away and took a large gulp of wine. That thousand-yard stare she had seen in the bar was back.

Chrissie went to the bathroom to clear her head. She was not so sure about Johnny now. The last thing she wanted was to deal with a drunk guy feeling sorry for himself after she finally decided to have sex for the first time since Mike broke her heart.

The buzz she felt kissing Johnny in the taxi had gone.

Chrissie walked back into the lounge. Johnny was passed out and snoring loudly.

'Oh, you are joking,' she said, looking at him with disgust and tears welling in her eyes. 'Thanks for nothing, Johnny. Thanks for nothing.'

*****

Mantra

Sophie Lyall and I grew up together on Whitby Street about half a mile from Northumberland Park. It had a lane that ran behind the houses where we could safely play football or just hang out because not many cars came down there during the day. Many of the families in the street had kids about the same age, so we got to know one another pretty well, and quite a few of us went to Christ Church C of E Primary School. It only took about 10 minutes to walk to school. It was fun. Splashing in the puddles was my favourite thing, although Sophie and the other girls did not find getting splashed as much fun as us boys did. No surprises there.

It was not all roses and chocolates in our street though. There were clashes at times. Next door to us was a family of four boys who became expert car thieves and small-time criminals. They did most of their crimes away from us thankfully. One of them was in my class and we got on okay. He was called Spike and I was never sure if that was his real name or not. I used to help him out with his homework sometimes so he left us alone. Spike's older brothers were scary individuals to look at, with loads of tattoos, and always looked angry.

Further down the street was a grumpy, old bugger we called Old Fartitus, who sometimes took special delight in turning his garden hose on us as we were walking past. My dad said he was harmless and to ignore him but there were stories he had been in prison, so we were wary of him. I never saw him smile.

Sophie lived two down from us and was the prettiest girl on Whitby Street. She had long, blonde hair in a ponytail until she was about 12 and then she just wore it layered which I really liked. She had a diamond smile but, despite her looks, was no pushover and definitely had no time for fools or attention seekers. As we got older into our teens, all the boys fancied her but she was not interested in them—or me in that way. She was attracted to brains it seemed, so we never had a chance. Her first boyfriend—when she was 16—was an intellectual type in his first year at university studying chemistry. None of us lads on the street could compete with him.

Sophie's parents and mine were close friends, so we ended up spending a lot of time together, which was cool, as we got along really well. I think if we had tried to have a relationship, it would have ruined our close bond, so I am pleased we have stayed best friends. Girlfriends and boyfriends have come and gone over the years but we have never changed how we are together. The odd partner of ours has questioned our relationship but there was never anything for them to worry about. We are soul mates, and that's always how we liked it.

Sophie is more than just a friend. She is a mentor to me, gives the best advice and never judges me. I battled through our teenage years with big, hopeful dreams that were unlikely to ever come to anything but she never set goals. It is only recently that I totally understand why that was. Unlike me, she never worried about the future or talked up what she wanted to do when she left school. It was always left open. Her core philosophy is: The simpler you make life, the better. She says too many people believe that to be happy, you have to always be chasing the next great achievement in your life or setting even more unrealistic, long-term goals. We are all taught that from a young age without even knowing it. Many times over the years, I have forgotten that sage advice.

Sophie and I see each other less these days than we used to. That's understandable, as we have different priorities and interests but we try to catch up at least every month. In between times, there are the calls, texts, emails and social media posts between us. We are as close as we ever were.

Last weekend, we went to Northumberland Park. It is our favourite space to hang out in with its herb gardens, sculptures and a bandstand we spent hours in when we were kids. It even has a pet cemetery, which is freaky if you ever read Stephen King's scary book *Pet Sematary*. The Glasshouse Tearoom serves up toasted cheese scones with loads of butter that I love. It has great views over a beautiful pond and we love the mature trees in autumn. Sophie says that you are never too old to enjoy walking through piles of fallen autumn leaves.

I had not had a great few weeks, so I was keen to talk to Sophie about stuff bothering me. Not for the first time I made the fatal mistake of forgetting that core philosophy she believed in. I came up with a stupid, throw-away line about getting lucky rather than focusing on what really matters.

'It is so hard trying to get ahead, you know, Sophie. Everyone I know seems to be doing better than me. I think if

I could just win some money on the lottery tonight, all my problems would disappear. Fat chance of that happening.'

It was said half in jest but Sophie was clearly frustrated by what I said. I guess after all the years we had talked about stuff, she expected better from me.

'Look, we are all desperate for positive outcomes and hoping that something good will come along to change our lives for the better, like winning the lottery or getting the best job imaginable. Life is just not like that for the vast majority of us, so we get let down all the time because those things don't happen to us. If you are always only looking out for those life-changing windfalls, or are influenced by others, that just sets you on the road to an unhappy life. What happens is we forget the great things happening right now, the gift of life that gets taken for granted.

'Don't worry about what others think of you. That's a mantra I say to myself every day. You should too. It will definitely change how you look at yourself, your self-esteem and your general happiness. It will put you in a far healthier place.'

Lecture over. She smiled at me and gave me a big hug. There was a fair bit to take on board but it all made sense as always. Some things take time to sink into my small brain.

The late autumn sunshine was starting to fade. We gazed out at the ducks floating on the pond without a care in the world. Sophie broke the spell with a request I never turned down.

'Hey, let's go and get a drink. Do you fancy a quick one at the Rock?'

The Rockcliffe Arms was a short five-minute drive away, just past Cullercoats Bay. It is another of our favourite haunts. It was a classic local pub, well away from the high street drinking parade and certainly not a place to go if you want top-quality nosh and trendy cocktails.

'A proper pub with no airs and graces, real beer and real people,' as my mate Dan once described it.

Sophie and I liked to go there about late afternoon. It was a great place to get away and find a quiet table and relax. Sarah, one of the old Whitby Street crowd, worked behind the bar and we just loved the friendly atmosphere. It was where I seemed to open up to Sophie easier than in more crowded and manic places we sometimes went to.

'I've been thinking about what you said earlier at the Glasshouse, Sophie. What you have made so clear to me, yet again, is I need to stop looking at the long-term picture, put myself first for a change and stop hoping the lucky numbers fall my way.'

Sarah was clearing glasses at the table next to us. She heard what I said.

'Sorry to eavesdrop but I couldn't help hearing. I agree with you. I have been trying to change too, not to become dependent on alcohol or drugs or be reliant on my boyfriend. He doesn't care for me or give a stuff about my needs or my emotions. He is really a maniac. Is that the right word, Sophie?'

'Yes, that sounds pretty accurate. You are doing so well now, Sarah. I'm so proud of you and how you have overcome so much.'

'Thanks. Means a lot coming from you, Soph. Well, I am determined to improve. My spirit and self-esteem is so much stronger now. I want to stay clean and sober for as long as it takes to get my life back on track. I live every day as it comes now. I am not looking too far ahead or giving a toss what others think. You know what? It is so liberating. This is the best I have felt for years, probably have to go back to those days playing in the street and having fun when we were kids.'

Sarah went back to the bar. Sophie went to the ladies. I stayed put at the table.

I thought about what we had talked about. I could now see I just needed to back myself, stop second-guessing everything I did and do what was best for me. I was going to get something positive out of every day.

That felt really good for a change.

*****

The Dying Light

The last orders bell startled me back to reality.

'Come on, people. Haven't you got homes to go to? Last drinks but be quick about it.'

Barman Charlie winked at me. I pushed my glass towards him. Even though the bar stayed open well into the early hours of Sunday morning, I was surprised it was that time already. Where had the last six hours gone?

I wanted one more whisky before I said goodbye to him for the last time.

'Stick one more in there. Cheers, mate.'

Charlie was always good to talk to. He may have thought I was a lost soul but he always listened to my ramblings and had some good advice at times. I was propped up on my usual stool at the end of the bar, away from everyone ordering, so I did not get hassled or bumped into by drunks but having the best view of the whole place.

I was usually on my own. Well, that's what anyone looking at me would think. But the reality was that the more whisky I drank, the more company I had. Two dead friends of mine often paid me a visit when I went from being mildly drunk to that period where your vision is blurred and you struggle to speak clearly. No one else could see Sally and Mikey but I could.

Sally and I went out for about two years. She was my first love and probably my closest friend. Even after we split up, we stayed in touch. Her death came completely out of some tragic left field no one could have anticipated. She was loved by everyone—pretty, intelligent and had started a new job with great prospects. That's what we all saw but not what Sally saw. We found out later she was stressed, suffering from chronic self-doubt and early stages of bulimia and had recently caught her boyfriend cheating on her.

When Sally had not shown up bright and early for breakfast one morning like she always did, her mum went into her room. Sally was dead, with an empty bottle of sedatives beside her and wine bottles on the floor. It was nearly 18 months ago, and it still hurts me big time. When I see her in my drunken state, she is always smiling, which numbs the pain for a second or two.

Mikey was someone I saw a lot of at school. We lived on the same street, so used to hang out. He was madly in love with this older, weird woman called Sandy, who took drugs and messed him around. It was nearly two years after we left school when she sent him a text saying she was finishing it. Whatever 'it' was meant far less to her than to Mikey, who always tended to wear his heart on his sleeve. I used to tell him she was bad news but he was having none of it. Smitten he was.

Mikey did not take the rejection well. A day after she dumped him, he hung himself in the backyard. His dad Mick found him, and he has not been right since. Sometimes I see Mick wandering the streets or in a bar. He looks totally bereft, like his will to live has gone. We don't have much to say to each other. What is there to say?

Getting through the night is our biggest test.

I had this diary I kept when I was 14. It was full of stuff a teenage boy can't talk to his parents, or mates or teachers about. Or so I thought at the time. Stuff like feelings and fears, doubts and mistruths, expectations and failures, self-loathing and second-guessing yourself over and over again.

At that time, I read a book about a guy my age who lived in New York and took his own life. Most of it was actually too intense for my young brain to comprehend but some of it resonated with me.

There was a four-line mantra he had written on the back of the book.

I can't take this shit anymore.
I don't want to live anymore.
Death is the only way out.
Someone take me out.

I got that. I wrote it on the inside cover of my diary. I saw it every day. I thought there was no way out of my despair and how I was feeling. It was like I was dying from the inside out, despite giving all the signs that I was still fine. As things got worse and I stopped sleeping much at night, I became increasingly more desperate. I even started to drop hints to the one teacher I trusted that I was in pain and struggling but the message got clouded somehow, probably because I was not clear enough. I should have just come out with it and said I was depressed and needed help.

But somehow, I survived those teenage years. I left school and got some part-time work doing basic labouring work with a builder. Then I got a job with EDS Newcastle serving customers and advising them about their electrical needs. It was about the only thing I was interested in. I had tinkered with fixing things in our garage at home for as long as I could remember. It was always me that sorted out the problem if a fuse blew or something was wrong with the boiler. Having a mechanical challenge to solve was the only time I forgot about being miserable when I was growing up.

The job was a saviour, to be fair. I am not saying I had everything sorted and under control, far from it, but finally I could see a future. Instead of wanting to end it all, I looked forward to seeing the morning light and going to work. It was a massive shift for me and I was happy for the first time in my life.

Then one night, I got the best news ever, ironically outside a shady bar. It was not my local, or anywhere I normally drank, but a mate of Mikey's I met at the funeral had asked me there. He organised some people who knew Mikey to have a few drinks to help try and make sense of it all. Not sure if it was a good idea but at least I found out what had happened leading up to him taking his life.

I went outside for a smoke. It was good to get out of there and try to clear my head a bit. One of the guys I had talked to in the bar was Paul Harrison. He came up to me and asked for a light. He was about my dad's age and turned out to be Mikey's godfather. Paul was the one who had told us about Mikey being dumped by Sandy.

'This is not easy to deal with for any of us. I'm really struggling to understand why he did that instead of talking to someone like me or his dad. God knows it must be tough for you and his younger mates.'

I nodded. I was still struggling with it all, so couldn't find any words, especially talking to a relative stranger. Paul gave me a moment and then came out with it.

'Look, I may be able to help you get over what has happened by giving you a new challenge to get your teeth into. I know your boss well at EDS. He tells me you are doing a good job, and you obviously know your stuff, but shop work is not really your thing. I am looking to take on another apprentice. I run an electrical company and business is going really well. Mikey always spoke highly of you as well. Why not come join me and kick-start a new career? What do you think?'

I looked at Paul. He was smiling and something about him made me feel at ease. I reckon I could trust this guy. This was the chance I had been waiting for.

'I don't know what to say. I have always wanted to get into the trades but never got round to doing anything about it. I guess I never thought anyone would take me on. I'd love to work for you and get an apprenticeship. Thanks, Paul.'

Getting through the night is our biggest test.

Two years later, just before my 22nd birthday, I was feeling positive about most things. I had not had a relapse into the dark world of depression since that chat with Paul. The apprenticeship was going well and I had started to think about what I could achieve once I was qualified. Maybe I could even set up my own business one day.

Then Covid happened and the economy and my life went downhill rapidly. Lockdown hit hard for me. Paul had to let me go, as he no longer had enough work for us all and could not afford to pay me. He promised he would have a job waiting for me when things picked up but he could not tell me when that would be. I quickly slid back into the black hole. After a few months without work, I started to wonder why I bothered to keep going and saw little point in most things. The black dog of depression that was always growling and barking at me during my teens began to bite me. When lockdown lifted enough to go to the mall, I started wearing a cap and sunglasses to hide behind. If I saw someone I knew in the street, I would cross the road before they saw me or lower my head, so all they saw was a cap and glasses. Mandatory masks—thank you, God. No one could recognise me.

I was just exhausted emotionally and physically tired all the time. Staring into space at home, confused by my irrational fears and not having a support network to lean on just made everything worse. I kept asking myself why this had happened now when I had finally turned my life around. Once the bars opened up again, I was seldom sober. It was a fatal combination of too much alcohol and too much focusing on the negative stuff. A good night's sleep was a rare thing for me. That two-year period working for Paul was the best time I had ever had, but now it was just a fading memory. Thanks for nothing, bloody Covid.

Getting through the night is our biggest test.

Charlie gave me the nod. It's time for me to go.

'See you soon, Sally and Mikey. I won't be long,' I said to myself as I finished my last drink.

I stumbled out of the bar. I knew what I was going to do. I had planned it in my mind for months since the worst of my depression returned after losing my job, but if I was being honest, I had thought about it for years. *Tonight's the night.* I remember that song by Rod Stewart my dad used to play all the time. He loved rocking Rod, me not so much, but that doesn't matter now.

The bar I left was 20 minutes from the massive Tyne Bridge that separates Newcastle and Gateshead. I read somewhere that the magnificent Sydney Harbour Bridge is based on the Tyne Bridge design, but history and great arches were the last thing on my mind as I reached the pedestrian walkway. I had ambled over the bridge hundreds of times and seen all the flowers left for the lost souls who silenced the noise in their heads.

Soon it will be all over for me too.

I don't know why I picked jumping off a bridge as the best, or easiest, or simplest or whatever bloody way to do it, but I did. Maybe just because it was always there and I saw it every day going to work. All I knew was I did not want to die in a plane crash. That really scared me. Now that's funny. I was scared to die in a plane but happy to jump off a massive bridge. Oh, the irony of it all!

There were only a few cars driving past on the bridge. It was getting on for 4:30 a.m., so just taxis and Ubers from what I could see. I took a deep breath and hopped over the protective railings and looked down for a moment. That made me shudder.

Shit, it's a long way down, I thought to myself.

The wind was biting cold, and despite all the whisky on board, I was shivering. I suddenly felt really uncomfortable. It seemed way harder than I thought it would be. Don't losers like me walk up here when they are pissed and just jump off without a care in the world? The honest truth is, it was horrible up there. I suddenly felt sober and scared. 'Help me, someone, please!' I started to cry.

Weird, random positive thoughts then began to flash through my mind.

I'm not sad, I'm not in pain, Paul has a job waiting for me, my mum's homemade shepherd's pie, my favourite cousin Tessa with the big smile, barman Charlie, Sally and Mikey, that girl I tried to chat up at the bar a few hours ago.

I took a deep breath. Dawn was breaking. The horizon lit up with a brilliant kaleidoscope of soft colours. I'd forgotten about the sheer majesty of a sunrise, especially from this high up. It stunned me back to reality. Suicidal thoughts had become my unwanted and constant companion for so long; they had worn down my will to live. Death had seemed like welcome relief, a peaceful end to all my pain. I had never been a religious person but on the bridge, something happened that I could not really explain away. Was that sudden, radical change in attitude and strong desire to live driven by a higher power? I think it was my Damascus moment for sure. I remember the story of Paul being converted from Judaism to Christianity while traveling the road to Damascus. It was my favourite Bible story and about the only one I remember from when I used to go to church to keep my mum happy.

Whatever the reason, I suddenly knew I could not go through with it. I wanted to get the hell off that bridge. I can't be that selfish and put all the people who love and care for me through what Sally and Mikey did. I thought of Mikey's dad Mick.

My Mum would never get over it if I jump. No, no, no. This stops now.

I walked back across the bridge, past the sign promoting the Samaritans if you are in despair, next to all the flowers. The mental stress I usually felt had lifted. I even smiled, just for a second but it was there. It took an hour or so to walk home, which gave me plenty of time to think things through and try to make sense of what had happened. I was so sure I was going to end it all and at the final moment, I realised I wanted to live. For once, my mind was uncluttered. A simple, clear mantra came to me instead—get well, get well, get well. I decided I would ask Paul if I could restart my apprenticeship. This positive energy was all new and felt a bit weird but I liked it.

I got home and went straight to bed. For once, the negative vibes and thoughts of doing myself in that kept me awake were not there. I slept for 10 hours. I woke up, and the sun was streaming through the windows in my room.

'Get well, get well, get well,' I chanted to myself.

Getting through the night is our biggest test.

*****

Angel in Lothian

I am fast asleep, aged 10. My magic dream is back again tonight. It always starts with bright lights that dazzle me as I try to work out what is happening and where I am. Just for a second, I feel afraid and then the lights fade to reveal a brilliant scene. Descending from the clouds is a beautiful angel with red, blue, orange and purple-coloured wings. She drifts down to the ground so slowly and looks over to me with big smile on her face. I wave out to her. The angel calls out me, 'Don't worry; everything will be alright.'

For a few seconds, there is complete silence and a tiful kaleidoscope of colours fills my dream. I feel safe arm. Suddenly, there is a loud explosion that makes me nd clouds of blue smoke. When the smoke clears, the s disappeared. I wait and wait but she doesn't come as sad as it gets for 10-year-old me. I need my angel. am then takes me back to our classroom at school. oto on the wall of a big white international space lack glass windows. I like the space station. It is y and looks cool with light reflecting off the ces of people I knew as a kid who have died ce station. I can see Uncle Bob and Aunt hbours Mary and Doug, plus the first dog we had when I was five, called Sandy. They are smiling at me, except for Sandy who is barking.

Next moment, I am standing at the back door of our house. It is dark and cold. I am trying to get in. I can't open the door. I bang and bang but it must be locked. There is a sound of something running. I don't know what it is but it is getting closer. I desperately try to open the door but it won't budge. Just as I start to scream, the dream is over. Many, many times I have woken upset and breathing hard. It gets me every time.

There is something special about being a kid. Mostly it is a happy time, a simple way of looking at the world around you and what happens every day. Back in my day, having fun meant doing things that didn't cost a cent, like playing with a ball outside, riding our bikes in the park or along the waterfront, doing stuff with our friends and looking forward to going to school. It really was a buzz at the start of a new term when you knew you would catch up with all your mates and see your favourite teacher again. That was a real natural high. Definitely better than the chemically induced ones I have had over the years.

I know I was happier and more energised in those early years before puberty ruined the innocence. It was all about living in the moment back then. As adults, we spend so much time unable to free ourselves from our mobile phones, worrying about that appointment scheduled for next week, financial problems, emotional turmoil, keeping our partner happy or solving the world's problems.

I like to remember those less complicated days. Life was good for me as a kid. What happened to my angel in Lothian after she landed was about all I had to worry about. My fertile imagination used to come up with weird and whacky creatures, spooky ghosts, imaginary friends and my own super heroes. It was all inspired by my brilliant teacher Miss McDonald, who inspired me to be creative like no one else did. She taught us about exciting myths and legends full of amazing characters like King Arthur, but some of them were quite scary too. Well, they were for me anyway. She also told us cool stories. Miss McDonald always made everything seem so exciting to me and the stories stuck in my imagination long after school had finished for the day.

Lothian and Bernicia were two of the old places we learnt about in school that had influences from Roman, Pictish, British, Gaelic and Anglo-Saxon cultures. There was a big map in our classroom with loads of coloured arrows pointing to these places we had never heard of with unusual names. Edinburgh is the only one I remember from those areas we know today as South-East Scotland and North-East England. One day, Miss McDonald told us a legend about an angel in Lothian who came down to Earth to stop the battles raging in the region between the huge armies trying to claim the areas of Lothian and Bernicia. That was the start of where my dream came from, with my imagination putting the bits and pieces together. There is no obvious link between it all. What does it all mean? I get some of it but not how it all fits together. It surely makes no sense, but does it have to? I have talked to a psychologist at times over the years about my dream. He says recurring dreams often indicate symptoms of anxiety and depression, which I have suffered from all my life. So there is that.

I grew up in Newcastle, so the Toon is my football team, but because of my special angel in Lothian, I have always had a soft spot for Edinburgh's Heart of Midlothian football club. Most people know them as Hearts. They are my second favourite team and I follow how they are doing in the Scottish Premiership. In another connection to Lothian, my wife— Shelley—is from Edinburgh. We met at the Strawberry Pub, right next to St James' Park. It was a typical heaving pre-match crowd. There was hardly room to swing a cat, let alone meet my future wife, but that's exactly what happened. I spotted Shelley at the table next to where I and a few mates were getting pints down us before we went next door to the Liverpool match. She looked cute and was wearing a Newcastle top, so that made her even more of a catch.

She made the first move actually. She came over to me and introduced herself.

'Hi, I'm Shelley. We are going across early now to get our seats but do you fancy meeting up later? I could meet you back here after the match if you fancy it.'

Did I what? We hooked up after beating Liverpool and just clicked straight away. It was a whirlwind romance. She seemed to understand me better than any other girl had, but that was not saying much. I'd never had much luck romantically—just happy to have occasional one-night stands mostly. I was more interested in football and getting pissed, to be fair. Shelley changed my life in so many positive ways but I didn't realise it until it was too late.

She grew up in Edinburgh, well away from the tourist traps of Princess Street, the Royal Mile and Edinburgh Castle. Her family lived near Great Junction Street in the northern part of the city. Her mum was tragically killed in a car accident when she was 13, leaving Shelley and her younger brother to be raised by her heartbroken dad. He became a chronic alcoholic who then struggled to look after his kids and hold down regular work. When she was 16, she and her brother left Edinburgh to live with her nan in Newcastle. At first, her dad tried to get them to come home but eventually he gave up. To be fair to him, he never missed sending birthday and Christmas cards but they did not see much of him in the years after they left.

When Shelley was 20, her dad walked into the side of a bus after a heavy session at his local pub—the Fox's Bar. He died a few hours later. She felt more numb than upset. How do you grieve for someone who was a nightmare to live with and caused so much upset when you were a teenager but was still your dad? She felt guilty that she was not more upset but the overriding emotion was relief that he was gone.

We got married when we were 22. The one thing she insisted on was that I cut back my drinking, as she worried I might end up like her dad. She told me a lot of stories about him. I promised I would. I said she had nothing to worry about, as I could cut back at any time, or so I thought. Little did I know that the seeds of alcoholism were already planted in my brain. The binge drinking on weekends had been a part of my life since I was 18 but I did slow down after we were married. We were happy for 20 months or so. Then all my old insecurities began to play up again. I could not believe I deserved Shelley and my lack of self-esteem began to play havoc with our relationship. She did really well at her career, while I went from job to job. My drinking got worse.

Things had not been great between us for a while. I had lost that cocky bravado and cheeky smile she first liked about me. Instead, I had become a bit of a miserable bastard and was drinking too much and too often. I had broken the promise I made to her. A week before our fifth wedding anniversary, I went on one bender too many. I had gone out with some old school mates. Quite a few pubs and clubs later, I turned up at our rented place as the morning papers were being delivered to the corner shop across the road. I felt like shit, smelt bad and had blood down the front of my shirt. I couldn't tell you if it was mine or not. I stumbled into the bins, sending them crashing loudly on the footpath. As I put my key in the lock, the front door opened. It was Shelley. She went inside without saying a word. I followed her in to the kitchen.

'Look at the state of you. Are you proud of yourself?'

I opened my mouth to answer and stopped. Proud of myself? No, I was not and never had been. The question lingered in my addled brain. Had anyone ever been proud of me? Finally, the words started to flow randomly as tears welled up in my bloodshot eyes.

'Shelley, let me explain. I am so sorry. I always mess things up. I won't do it again. I will change, Shelley. You know me; I just stuff things up. I wish I could turn the clocks back but I can't. I'm really sorry. I know I mucked up again but I will change. I promise. Please give me one more chance, Shelley.'

She looked at me with sadness and pity. I had never seen that look from her. Usually it was pure anger in her eyes. She would yell and swear at me. Then after a few hours, we would start to find some middle ground and rebuild our relationship. But this time felt different. She said nothing at first and just looked at me like I was a badly behaved puppy who had pissed on the carpet.

When she started talking, her voice was calm and controlled. Every word was like a dagger to my heart and ripped apart the last remnants of our broken marriage.

'You have hurt me once too often. Last night lying in our bed, waiting for you to come home, I never felt so alone. I had no idea where you were, who you were with, if you were alright or had been beaten up or run over staggering across the road. When we got married, you said you would stop drinking as much. I believed you. I really wanted to believe you because our future depended on you holding up your end of the bargain.

'You know more than anyone how hard it was for me growing up. I said when I am with you, I don't feel scared anymore. I don't feel lonely anymore. That's all changed now. I am sick of worrying, sick of being lied to, sick of caring actually. It's over between us. Go back to whoever you were with last night or whatever bar you were in. I really don't care anymore. Just leave me alone.'

The end of our marriage was predictable but so avoidable if I had focused on Shelley's needs, on us and our future and laid off the booze. But I was too selfish and wallowing in self-pity to see the big picture. The worst thing was that I really loved Shelley and still do. I might get lucky again and meet someone like her but I probably won't. There is still a chance we can make a go of it but I have to convince her I have changed. There is a long journey to go but I am trying. Ironically, since I moved in with my mate Deano six months ago, I have actually been doing what Shelley wanted. I have cut back the drinking and am trying to feel better about myself.

But the main problems will not leave me alone—my lack of self-esteem and mild depression. Most of the time I can handle it, and the right medication really helps, but my dark moods are never far away. It gets me down.

What I really need is my angel in Lothian to again slowly float down to me and tell me, 'Don't worry; everything will be alright.'

*****

Printed in the USA
CPSIA information can be obtained
at www.ICGtesting.com
CBHW071535230724
12052CB00006B/134